WHY THIS IS AN EASY READER

- This story has been carefully written to keep the young reader's interest high.

- It is told in a simple, open style, with a strong rhythm that adds enjoyment both to reading aloud and silent reading.

- There is a very high percentage of words repeated. It is this skillful repetition which helps the child to read independently. Seeing words again and again, he "practices" the vocabulary he knows, and learns with ease the words that are new.

- Only 179 different words have been used, with plurals and root words counted once.

  Over one-half of the total vocabulary of this story has been used at least three times.

  Over one-fourth of the total vocabulary of the story has been used at least six times.

  Some words have been used 11, 17 and 22 times.

ABOUT THIS STORY

- Here is one of the most interesting examples of protective coloration in nature. The snowshoe rabbit, as this story shows, adapts constantly to the changing landscape in which he lives. The young reader will begin, of course, by caring about worried Benny Bunny, who doesn't understand yet what is happening to him. But he can be led very easily from this story to a real interest in the marvelous ways in which living creatures adapt to their environments.

The Three Coats of
BENNY BUNNY

Story by SARA ASHERON
Pictures by ELIZABETH DAUBER
Editorial Consultant: LILIAN MOORE

Wonder® Books
ALLAN PUBLISHERS, INC.
Exclusive Distributors

Introduction

These books are meant to help the young reader discover what a delightful experience reading can be. The stories are such fun that they urge the child to try his new reading skills. They are so easy to read that they will encourage and strengthen him as a reader.

The adult will notice that the sentences aren't too long, the words aren't too hard, and the skillful repetition is like a helping hand. What the child will feel is: "This is a good story—and I can read it myself!"

For some children, the best way to meet these stories may be to hear them read aloud at first. Others, who are better prepared to read on their own, may need a little help in the beginning—help that is best given freely. Youngsters who have more experience in reading alone—whether in first or second or third grade—will have the immediate joy of reading "all by myself."

These books have been planned to help all young readers grow—in their pleasure in books and in their power to read them.

Lilian Moore
Specialist in Reading
Formerly of Division of Instructional Research,
New York City Board of Education

1981 PRINTING

Cover Copyright © 1981 GROSSET & DUNLAP INC.

Text Copyright © 1968 by Sara Asheron.

Illustrations Copyright © 1968 by Grosset & Dunlap, Inc.

All rights reserved under International and Pan-American Copyright Conventions.

Published simultaneously in Canada. Printed in the United States of America.

Published by GROSSET & DUNLAP, INC.

Exclusively distributed by Allan Publishers, Inc.

Wonder® Books is a trademark of GROSSET & DUNLAP, INC.

ISBN: 0-8241-5952-7

Benny was a little rabbit.

Some rabbits live on a farm.

Some rabbits live

in a pet shop.

Sometimes a rabbit lives in a house
with a boy or girl.

Benny Bunny did not live

on a farm.

He did not live in a pet shop

or in a house.

Benny Bunny was a snowshoe
rabbit, and he lived
in the cold, cold Northland.

A snowshoe looks like this:

A man can walk on deep, deep snow
with snowshoes.

A snowshoe rabbit has feet like this:

So a snowshoe rabbit looks as if
he has little snowshoes on his feet.

Snowshoe rabbits can hop
and run fast on the winter snow
in the Northland.

But it was summer now

in the Northland, and it was

Benny Bunny's first summer.

In the summer

the ground in the Northland

looks brown.

Benny Bunny's coat was brown, too.

Brown as the ground.

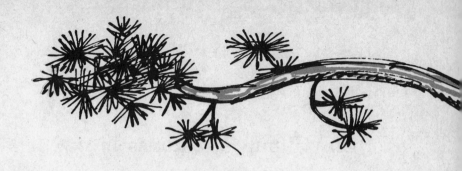

Benny Bunny was little,

and he liked to run and play.

But he had to watch out—

all the time.

He had to watch out for Old Owl.

He had to watch out for Fox.

And he had to watch out

for Big Bear.

They all wanted to catch

a fat little snowshoe rabbit.

Benny Bunny was not afraid.

He could run fast.

He could hide in a little brown bush.

No one could see a little brown
rabbit in a little brown bush.

 One day, Big Bear saw

Benny Bunny playing.

Big Bear called out,

"Now I will get you!"

Benny Bunny ran.

How he ran!

He ran into a little brown bush.

Big Bear looked around.

"Where is that rabbit?"

said Big Bear.

"I saw him here just now!"

He did not see

the little brown rabbit

in the little brown bush.

"Some day I will catch him!"

said Big Bear.

And he went away.

"I have a good coat!"

thought Benny Bunny,

and he was not afraid.

But one day his mother said,

"Soon the summer will be over,

Benny Bunny,

and you will be getting a new coat.

Just in time, too!"

Poor Benny Bunny.

A new coat!

"What will I do with a new coat?"

he thought.

"How will I hide from Owl

and Fox and Bear?"

Soon it was colder in the Northland.

Colder and colder.

Here and there, some snow
began to fall.

One day Mother Rabbit said,

"I can see your new coat growing in.

I can see some white hairs."

Poor Benny Bunny.

"What will I do, now?"

he thought.

"What will I do now?"

Soon Mother Rabbit said,

"I see more white hairs in your coat.

Your new coat is brown and white.

And it is growing fast."

Benny Bunny thought about Owl.

He thought about Fox and Big Bear.

And he did not go out to play.

But one day, he had to go out.

He had to look for food

with Mother Rabbit.

On the way home, they saw Fox.

"Run!" cried Mother Rabbit.

Benny Bunny and his mother ran.

How they ran!

They ran into a little bush.

"Be very still!" said Mother Rabbit,

"and Fox will not find us!"

"He will!" cried Benny Bunny.

"My coat is brown and white now.

He will see me!"

"Look around you, Benny Bunny,"
said his mother.

Benny Bunny looked around.

He was so surprised.

The Northland was brown and
white now!

Here and there,
he saw brown bushes.

Here and there,
he saw white snow.

Benny Bunny was so happy.
The Northland was brown and
white, and so was his new coat.

He ran out to play again—all day.

"No one can catch me!"

thought Benny Bunny.

"No one can catch me now!"

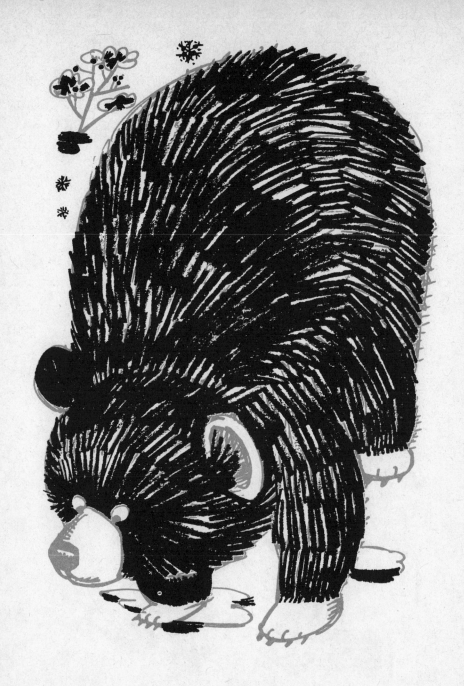

One day, Big Bear ran after him.

But the little rabbit

ran into a bush to hide.

"Where is that rabbit?"

said Big Bear.

"I saw him here just now!"

But he could not see

a brown-and-white rabbit

in a brown-and-white bush.

So Big Bear went away.

"I have a good coat!"

thought Benny Bunny,

and he was not afraid.

It was very, very cold
in the Northland now.
"Soon it will be winter,"
said Mother Rabbit one day.
"Benny Bunny, your new coat
is growing in.
And just in time!"

A new coat!

"Oh, no!" thought Benny Bunny.

"I don't want a new coat.

The one I have is just right."

And he was afraid again.

Benny Bunny would not go out.

Day after day, he stayed inside.

"Come out with me,"

said Mother Rabbit.

"Not today," said Benny Bunny.

Soon Mother Rabbit said again,

"Come out with me."

And Benny Bunny said again,

"Not today."

Then his mother said, "What is it,
Benny Bunny? What is the matter?"
And he told her.
"I'm afraid," he said.
"I'm afraid of my new coat."

"Benny Bunny," said his mother.

"Look at me.

Look at my new coat."

Benny Bunny saw now that

his mother's coat was all white.

"Your new coat is white
and pretty, too," said his mother.
A white coat!
Benny Bunny began to cry.

"Don't be afraid, Benny Bunny,"
said his mother.

"You have a good coat.

And look at your feet!"

Benny Bunny

was surprised to see

that he had big snowshoe feet.

"See!" said his mother.

"You are ready now."

"Ready?" said Benny Bunny.

"Ready for what?"

"Come and see," said his mother.

"Look outside."

Benny Bunny looked outside

and cried "OH!"

What a surprise!

The world was white with snow.

Everything was white,

white as his new coat.

"See!" said his mother.

"You have snowshoe feet

and a snow-white coat.

You are ready for the

Northland winter."

"Well, come on!"

cried Benny Bunny.

"Let's go! Let's go!"

And he ran out

into the snow-white world.